HOW TO LAND AN EAGLE

JOEL CROFOOT

PERMISSIONS AND CREDITS

PROLOGUE

"**M**aybe this was a bad idea."

Her sister's voice, muffled by the distance, drifted down from the haymow.

"This was the only idea that had a chance of success, and it is totally going to work."

Rachel looked around at the filthy barn, currently being emptied of its occupants as the horses meandered out to pasture, and wished she had her sister's confidence. It would need to be cleaned, lights hung, a stage built, and the sound system set-up, and they only had a day to do it all.

"Hey look!" Deanna called as she descended the ladder. "If we have the shifters come down from the haymow when it's their turn, the first thing the audience would see is their back. It adds to the intrigue." The dark haired woman jumped the last few rungs, landing on the soiled concrete. "If we put the chairs all along here, and leave a walkway down the center, we could put the stage right there, and maybe even a bar over there. Or..." her excitement was bubbling over, "...we could put chairs out in the driveway, facing the barn, and use this as a cat walk! Maybe we could even make bleachers from hay bales so everyone can see!"

Rachel raised her eyebrows and took a deep breath to steady her nerves. Her little sister was in full event-planning mode, while her son was in the hospital an hour away. He was getting a transfusion that would buy him another six months of childhood. Rachel hoped it was six this time. The transfusions became more and more frequent as the disease progressed.

Kevin had been diagnosed at the age of ten with uniform shifter's disease, a blood disorder that would eventually prevent him from shifting between his animal and human forms, but it wasn't certain which state he would ultimately remain as. From what the doctors could tell, by the age of twenty-five he would be limited to one form, unable to reproduce, and would have a shortened life span.

Rachel checked her watch, wondering if she should call her husband and ask how everything was going, but based on the time, they might not even have started the procedure yet.

"Rachel." Deanna's voice broke into her thoughts.

"Yeah?"

"The doctor said they're on the verge of a breakthrough. The money we raise from this auction is going to raise more than enough for all that equipment and the fancy researcher they need to hire. I know you want to be there, but you are helping here too."

She nodded, mostly just to acknowledge that she'd heard what was said, because she had her doubts about how much they could raise at an auction for a date with a shifter. What if no one showed up? What if they did and thought they were in the wrong place because she hadn't had time to attend to the farm lately?

She looked around again at the work that needed to be accomplished. Had they bitten off more than they could chew? Could two people even shovel all this bedding out in one day?

A cloud of dust, beyond the open barn door at the end of the long drive, caught her attention. "Is someone here? Probably those damn debt collectors," she hissed, grabbing a pitch fork as she walked out of the barn, intending to run them off. Then she stopped short when she recognized the vehicle was the first of a small convoy.

The leader of the local wolf shifter pack drove the red pickup truck in the front, followed by cars from the bear, lynx, and panther clans. Above them an eagle circled, and then a crow and a burst of flame announced the arrival of the dragons. Clouds of dust from the dirt road indicated even more people on the way.

Rachel panicked, feeling her breath catch in her throat at the idea that they'd all see her completely unprepared. "What's going on? They weren't supposed to be here until tomorrow! We're not ready!"

"I invited them."

The red truck parked and more animals came scurrying out of the truck-bed and started shifting into human form.

"Why would you do that? We have so much that needs to be done. We can't be entertaining pack leaders." Dammit, her younger sister could be so irresponsible at times.

Rachel felt her jaw clench as a dragon dropped into the field behind Deanna, scattering the livestock to the far corners.

"Mrs. Gavin?" a man asked as he approached.

Initially she stood frozen, concerned more about her horses, then whoever was calling her, but when the dragons shifted form and began to approach the barn, leaving the horses alone in the pasture, the tension in her shoulders eased. It might be silly to worry, but she hadn't had any dealings with dragons before.

She turned her eyes towards the local Alpha before her. He was a handsome man, his face decorated with a gray-speckled, trimmed beard, and dark eyes.

"Yes."

"We heard about the auction to raise money for research into Uniform Shifters Disease, and a little birdy told us you might need help." He winked at Deanna as he mentioned the last part. "We're at your disposal for any and all preparations that you may need."

Her mouth fell open as she looked between her sister and this chieftain as she processed what he'd just said.

"I... um... Yes, sir. But why would you do this?"

He smiled warmly, reaching out to take the pitchfork from her. "This disease affects us all and if you're going to do something about it, so are we."

* * *

"This is amazing! I can't believe it." Rachel and Deanna knelt at the little window of the haymow, overlooking the front entrance to their red barn. Below them hay bales were stacked in a semi-circle around the wide barn door entrance to provide seating enough for at least a hundred people. They'd even used old grain bags to line the ones they could in case anyone was foolish enough to try to sit on hay in shorts or a skirt.

Rows of hanging lights were strung from the top of the barn to the bleachers giving a nice patio feel to the atmosphere. The animal feed trough had been filled with ice to keep drinks cool and placed behind a newly constructed bar, and behind them in the haymow the shifters were dressing for the auction.

"This is going to be awesome!" Deanna said, as she ushered Rachel back from the window and climbed off the hay stack that had been supporting them. "So the shifters will come down the ladder from the haymow, the DJ will play music as they walk to the doorway of the barn where the audience can see them, and once they enter the spot light, the auctioneer will start the bidding." As if on cue the man began testing his microphone, just as cars started to pull into the drive. "Let's get down there."

Rachel and Deanna walked past the dozens of handsome men and women who had volunteered to be auctioned off for 'a date for a night' to raise funds. They smiled as the women passed, and Rachel wished she could individually hug them all for agreeing to this. She knew they all had their reasons too. Almost every shifter knew at least one person affected by the disease and gaining this money would go a long way to help.

"How did you get the word out about this?" Rachel asked when they were down the ladder and walking towards the front.

"Social media," Deanna answered nonchalantly. "We marketed it as a popup auction, and the Summerton gazette picked it up, and then it just went viral."

"Oh wow, so we're going to have a bunch of city slickers here too?"

Deanna threw her a grin. "That's where the money is, right?"

Rachel proudly studied her little sister for a moment. "I'm sorry I ever doubted you."

Deanna playfully nudged her with her elbow. "Yeah, you'll grow out of it. Come on, let's grab a seat."

Soon they were sitting in the front row, surrounded by strangers who were piling onto the bleachers with paper numbers to wave if they wanted to bid. The back of the bid card also held a docket of the line-up of shifters expected.

"How long were you really planning this?" Rachel asked, seeing the list of shifters and piecing together that some had to come from other continents.

"About six months."

"And you just told me yesterday!"

Deanna laughed. "You had enough on your plate. Besides,

if I'd told you about this any sooner you would have had time to back out. You worry too much."

Now that was a fair accusation.

Music from the DJ began before she could reply and the audience quickly found their seats as the auctioneer introduced himself. He explained the cause, gaining a round of cheers from the crowd.

"So without further ado, ladies and gentlemen, our first shifter for the night is…"

***

Author note: This prologue was written for a shared world within the Shifter's Unleashed collection. Please keep reading to learn more about one shifter's story.

CHAPTER 1

Wanbli Daniels didn't expect to feel nervous for the event, but here he was, standing in a hay loft, waiting for his turn to be auctioned off like a piece of meat.

Why did I do this to myself? he thought, but then he remembered the look on Rachel's face when they'd all shown up to pitch in. It was something between awe and gratitude, and with all the money going towards research into uniform shifter's disease, taking a stranger on a date was the least he could do. Unlike some others waiting their turn, that was the only reason he was here, *he* didn't need help to find a date.

He didn't want to date actually. He was more of a friends-with-benefits kind of guy.

No, that's a lie, I want to date, I just shouldn't.

The thought made him sad, and he sighed inwardly before he returned to listening to the auctioneer.

Luckily for him, he'd tuned back in at just the right time, and he heard his name announced.

Well here goes nothing…

He started to climb down the ladder, listening to the crowd cheer as he descended and tried his best to mimic models on a catwalk while he strode toward the front of the barn, a behavior that he would have been embarrassed to admit he'd actually practiced! When he stepped into the spotlight the sounds of excited female cheering grew, but the light shining in his eyes prevented him from seeing clearly into the stands.

Instead, he caught the beat of the music playing, tucked his thumbs in his jeans and did a little spin on his heels so he was no longer facing the crowd. His confidence grew with whistles and encouraging shouts, he pumped his hips a few times, and then turned back, continuing his best impression of a stripper, and praying that the audience couldn't tell how embarrassed he really was. The bidding had started and was climbing high as he ran his flat palm up his body from his pelvis to chest, then pointed at the crowd in time with the beat he was keeping in rhythm to. Placing a hand on his hip he gave the crowd a few sexy circles and listened as the bidding shot up.

Finally, after what felt like a thousand years, but was probably only a few minutes, he heard the blessed cue that he could cease this act he was putting on.

"Going once, going twice, sold to bidder 39!"

With a relieved exhale he winked in the direction he thought the winning bid had come from and exited the spotlight for the side of the barn, as the others had done before him.

"Nice moves," came an amused exclamation from his friend Garrett, who approached with a cold bottle of water.

"Thanks," Wanbli answered, snatching the water and chugging it all. "Who got me?"

"That cute little Asian woman on the far left. From what I've seen you're the only one she's bid on tonight," he added with an arched eyebrow and a smirk. "She must have a thing for feathers. Hey, maybe she's ticklish!"

Wanbli snorted. "Why am I friends with you?"

"You have a thing for fur. It's OK, everyone has a kink. Don't deny your attraction to me."

"Ugh huh." Wanbli answered flatly. "So who got you?"

CHAPTER 2

Amy couldn't believe she'd just spent hundreds of dollars to bid on a man, let alone a man she was betting was a serial killer. She took a deep breath to calm herself and glanced around self-consciously, hoping no one noticed how nervous she seemed. She tried to drag her checkbook out of her purse and found that even her hands were shaking as she imagined the ways she may die at his hands.

Don't think about it, what was I doing?

Oh right.

Seven hundred dollars to catch a serial killer! If this doesn't win me a Pulitzer I'm going to quit, she thought, even as she recognized that it was a lie.

She couldn't quit.

She imagined driving her little red sedan the hundreds of miles back to the trailer park she grew up in, with her metaphorical tail between her legs. All the neighbors staring at her from their windows, and then starting the gossip train, spreading their opinions about what happens to folks with dreams bigger than their talent. Her high school teacher, Mrs.

Smalman, would be proven right when she'd told her that she'd never amount to anything.

She felt her cheeks flush with humiliation and shame at the thought of returning home.

She'd have to face all of her classmates whose parents could afford college, the ones who made fun of her for walking around with her nose in books.

Screw them, and screw Mrs. Smalman.

The worst thing, though, would be the look on her dad's face. He'd spent his whole life taking care of her after her mother had walked out on them. He'd worked long hours to feed her, taking on a second job, to pay the bills, and always telling her that she could be happy, rich and successful someday.

And she wasn't going to let him down.

She was going to make it big, even if she had to spend her savings to buy herself dinner with a serial killer and live on dried noodle soup for months until after the story broke.

If she lived through this at all that was.

* * *

Amy returned home after leaving her name and a number (not her real one) for her date when she dropped off the check.

Three flights of stairs later, she flicked on the lights to her studio apartment and walked in, locking the door behind her. An empty feeling in her stomach reminded her that she couldn't exist on coffee alone, so she opened the fridge, despite already being aware of how empty it was. She had to settle on a plain bagel.

She needed to go grocery shopping but that might have to wait until her next paycheck, so bagels and coffee would have to sustain her until then.

It could be worse, she reminded herself. I could be back home in a smoky trailer.

As she chewed, she wandered over to the table, currently doubling as a desk, which was covered with newspaper clippings about the local serial killer the cops were looking for. Some of the pictures of the crime scenes she'd managed to get with her long-range camera lenses – which was the most expensive items she owned– other articles came off the internet, all helped her with some of her theories.

The killer thus far attacked both men and women in seemingly random fashion. None of the victims knew each other, and of the six, there was a vast difference in economic status. Nothing was taken from the bodies so robbery was out of the question. The only connection was that all the victims were shifters, though all different animals, and that they had been killed in the same fashion - gouging their eyes, then stabbing them with a blade.

The forensic examiner's theory was that there was something psychological about the eyes to the killer, like maybe the victims had seen something they shouldn't have, or the killer had an obsession with eyes, but Amy had a different theory.

She'd grown up a far cry from the city, and she'd seen how birds of prey attacked small animals, puncturing their skulls and gouging their eyes at the same time. Her guess was that this was a shifter raptor that gouged eyes then shifted and finished them off with the knife. She'd done some digging at the local shifter guilds and clubs and found out that there was one raptor shifter who'd just moved to the city around the times the killing had started.

And she had a date with him.

CHAPTER 3

W anbli was dressed in black slacks and a black silk button down shirt that contrasted nicely with his pure white hair. The hair made him look older than he was, but in truth he'd had white hair since he was about fifteen. It was part of being a bald eagle shifter. He'd never been self-conscious about it, if anything it helped him get better paying jobs when he was young.

The black, trimmed beard that accented his face was the color of his feathers and really gave him away as a bald eagle – to those who knew to look. He'd even done some acting jobs for a series of patriotic themed beer commercials a few years ago.

Now however, he stood back from the full length mirror as he finished buttoning his cuffs and gave himself a once over. He looked good, but part of him wished he didn't.

What am I doing?

He shook his head. *It's alright to date, I'm just doing this for the charity remember. I need a treatment, we all need it, he reminded himself. Just don't get attached and don't let her get attached.*

"No attachments," he said aloud, and took a deep breath to steel himself against the possibility of feelings.

"But since I have to do this, I might as well make the best of it."

my stood outside the fancy Italian restaurant in a little black dress that hid the shorts underneath and her well-worn flats, in case she had to flee at any point in the night. Her date had offered to pick her up, but she wasn't about to get in a vehicle with someone she suspected was a serial killer.

When she saw him walking up on the sidewalk, her heart almost flipped at the sight of someone so handsome and so sharply dressed. He was built like a gymnast with broad shoulders and a narrow waist, and she could see the power in him just by the way he strode toward her, like he was holding himself back. The suit he was wearing must have been tailored for him because it seemed to accentuate every muscle in his body.

He was a predator, and confidence oozed from him.

Stop ogling him. This is just work. You can't like him, it could get you killed. Stay focused, you need a raise.

Her automatic smile faded too late, he'd seen it and waved.

"Hi!" he greeted as he approached. "Amy?"

"Hi, yes. And you're Waaan…" She trailed off, not sure she was pronouncing his name correctly.

"Wanbli, yes. Shall we go in? We have reservations."

Soon they were seated in a small booth that was too dark for her liking, but at least they were in public.

"So thanks for bidding on me," he said, as soon as they were seated. "I hope I can live up to your expectations for a date."

I hope I can live! "I'm sure you will," she replied, placing her napkin on her lap. "So what do you shift into?" she asked.

"I'm a bald eagle shifter, that's also what my name means, eagle," he spoke, flashing dark handsome eyes her way.

Smokin' hot! Why does he have to be a serial killer? "In what language?"

"Lakota, but I'm not Native American. My family likes to collect the word 'eagle' in various languages and assigns them as names," he answered with a little chuckle, that revealed a hint of straight white teeth between his full lips. "My father's name is Adelaar, which is Dutch for eagle."

Stop checking out the murderer.

Forcing a smile she asked, "And what do you do as a human?"

"I'm a pilot for a company with a few wealthy private owners. I guess flying just comes naturally for eagles."

A pilot? She hadn't expected that. She set down the menu she'd been casually perusing. "Does that mean you travel a lot?"

He nodded his head and clasped his hands in front of him on the table. "Unfortunately yes, well actually it comes and goes depending on their schedules. For the last month I was gone more often than not, but I don't have anything on the calendar for this month."

"Wait, were you gone on the fourth?" she asked, already spotting a potential hole in her theory.

He gave her a baffled look, then adjusted his eyes up and to the side as he tried to recall. "Yeah, that whole week I was in Europe. Why, did I miss something?"

Dammit! She felt like such a fool. She'd just spent hundreds of dollars for a date with this man to blow the lid off the serial killer story and he wasn't even in town when it happened.

"What's wrong?" he interjected into her pity-party. "You look upset. Did I miss something on that date?"

"I, um, think I… um…" She tried to come up with a way to say 'Thought you were a serial killer' in a manner that didn't sound like she was accusing him of killing people, but couldn't find anything. "Just remembered I left something plugged in at home."

"Oh no. Should we reschedule?" he asked, looking all earnest and making her feel even worse about lying and thinking he was a sociopath.

She shook head. "No, it's nothing important."

"Okay." He paused, studying her a moment like he wasn't sure what to say. "What about you?" he asked, glancing down at the menu and back up. "What do you do?"

That's right, I'm supposed to pick food. She tried to skim the list and respond at the same time. "I work for the Channel Five News."

"Wow! That's a cool job. Sorry if I was supposed to recognize you, I don't really get to watch a lot of the news."

"It's alright. No one recognizes me, I'm not famous yet." The truth was that she was more like the fact-checker, the coffee retriever, more than the in-front-of-the-camera talking head, but with a case like this, she could change it.

They were silent as the waiter returned to pour glasses of red wine, and then Wanbli picked up his glass and offered her a toast. "To being famous someday."

This time she smiled brightly and lifted her glass to return the toast. Studying him while she took her sip, she finally let herself drink in the image of a sexy shifter in front of her that probably wasn't any more dangerous than other men, and who after knowing her for ten minutes already believed she could be famous someday.

CHAPTER 5

Wanbli watched the woman take a sip of wine, and at last felt himself relaxing a little. *Finally, I got a smile out of her. Up until now she'd seemed so cold.*

"So what's good here?" she asked, gesturing toward the menu.

"I really like the trout personally, but I think everything is good here. To be fair, eagles really like fish."

She laughed this time then sipped her wine again and finally let her shoulders drop. "Do you come here often?"

"Usually once a week when I'm in town," he answered.

"So you date a lot then?"

Oh shit, here it comes. "Not a lot." The truth was he went out on a lot of dates with a lot of different women and he slept with a lot of different women, and none of them stuck around. Either they ran away as soon as they found out about the disease he carried, or he ran them off for their own good.

"Then what made you join the auction?" she asked.

This time he picked up his glass and took a decent drink. "I believe in the cause." He was saved from further explanation by the waiter returning again and taking their order, but unfortunately she picked up where it had been interrupted.

"Yes, the disease is pretty sad. Do you know anyone with it?"

And here it is… the end of the date.

He took another drink and nodded. "Yeah, my dad has it; he's stuck as a human." He debated on telling her the rest. If he didn't tell her he might get a second date, maybe even get laid, but it would be living a lie. Did he really want to do that?

No, he was done living that life, even if he never got laid again. "And even though I don't have it, I'm a carrier," he admitted.

Nervously, he studied her reaction as he killed his wine. She would be putting the pieces together. His kids could get it and he'd be dooming them, so he could never have kids, therefore he wasn't marriage material. The date would take an awkward turn; they'd text once or twice, and never see each other again.

Wanbli took a breath and really assessed the woman across from him to see her reaction. Usually, there was a telltale sign of her disappointment even if it was just a downward flick of the eye or leaning away from him.

She just nodded. "I'm sorry to hear that, but I'm glad you still get to talk to your dad. It must be hard for him, but I imagine if he was an eagle it would be more difficult for you."

Her lack of a reaction was baffling.

Maybe this really is just a date for charity to her. Something was different about her though, he'd done this enough times to know that women always fled when they learned he wasn't marriage material, if not, they usually turned out to be bat-shit crazy.

He tried to covertly examine her, analyzing everything for red flags of insanity.

That was the first time he really noticed how attractive she was. Her skin had a golden shimmer in the dim light and her dark eyes seemed to radiate a heat he hadn't noticed until now. Her complexion was smooth as the windswept sand dunes of the winter snow, but the lipstick she was wearing drew his eye to those sumptuous lips. A reflective sheen of gloss coated them and under the table he felt his cock stiffen with the idea of what those lips would look like coated with something else. He shifted uncomfortably trying to refocus his attention.

"So what about you?" he asked. "What brought you to the auction?"

She froze and her eyes grew wide.

She's about to reveal her crazy side… she can't get a date the normal way because she hears voices or she's into something really weird and kinky or…

"Honestly? I thought you were a serial killer."

Wanbli almost spit out the wine he'd sipped, and coughed the little that he had accidentally inhaled, before he could respond with 'What? Why? And why would you want to date a serial killer?' Fortunately, she began explaining anyway.

"You know that serial killer that's been murdering shifters for the last few months?"

His mouth fell open for a brief moment before he answered her. "What? No! There's a serial killer after shifters?!"

She raised her eyebrows in disbelief. "You haven't heard about it?"

"I don't watch the news, remember?"

She sat back and nodded. "Oh right, sorry. Yeah, there's a killer targeting shifters. He's gotten six so far."

"And you thought I was *him*?" His voice raised several octaves.

She cringed. "Sorry." She looked down. "It's just that it makes sense that it would be a raptor because of the way the killer gouges the eyes when he attacks them, and you moved to town right when the attacks started."

That last part gave him a pause. "How do you know when I moved here?"

Her cheeks darkened with a vivid blush. "I investigated with all the raptor shifter guilds, and you were the only one that registered around that time."

He wasn't sure if he should be angry or not. She was just investigating in general, not him specifically, at least not until the auction.

Or was she?

"So what else do you know about me?" he asked with a flirtatious smirk designed to cover up his trepidation that she might know that he had a reputation as a player.

She shrugged. "Just your name and address, but when I was searching for you on the internet I found the auction and decided that would be the perfect way to find out more." She offered an awkward smile. "But I see I was wrong about that now," she sighed dejectedly, "...which means I'm back to square one."

The waiter chose that time to deliver their food, and they paused the conversation.

"I'm sorry," she added, as soon as the waiter left.

He shook his head. "No need to apologize. You were just doing your job." He'd already decided to forgive her; he probably would have done the same thing if he was in her position. As they ate their first few bites, he pondered this news about a serial killer.

"You said they gouge the eyes of their victims?"

Oh wait, that isn't a very good dinner conversation subject, is it?

CHAPTER 6

Amy nodded excitedly as she finished chewing and withdrew her phone from her purse to pull up a picture. *If he isn't the killer it would be great to have a raptor as a consultant on this.*

She showed him the picture and he took the phone, using his fingers to enlarge it. She wished the quality was better, but it was just a photograph of a police photograph after all.

He pinched his lips. "It's hard to tell from this because there's so much blood that would be covering up the scratches from claws if it was a raptor. Did you get to see the body after the blood was washed off?"

"No, I wish. I have some better pictures at my apartment if you want to stop by after dinner though?"

I can't believe I just invited him to my place on the first date!

It's for work, you need him, she argued with herself.

"I'd love to," he replied and her stomach fluttered.

The rest of dinner was a blur as Amy debated internally, but the more she watched those muscles ripple under his shirt, and saw the heat in his dark eyes, the more reasons she found to justify inviting him to her place.

She pictured him pushing her lightly against a wall, his hands running up her torso, his breath on her lips…

Get back to the conversation Amy.

She'd completely lost the thread of it and had to improvise a comment about the restaurant and the service.

Finally, he paid the check. "Shall I give you a ride to your place, now that we've established I'm not a serial killer?" he joked.

She grinned. "Sure."

* * *

Wanbli tried to curb his expectations for the night. He wasn't sure if this was a coy way to get them into a private location, or if she really wanted his opinion on a serial killer. Either way, with a serial killer on the loose he didn't want her heading home alone. What if this was the one time the killer changed his MO to killing non-shifters?

He tried to keep his eyes to himself as they climbed the stairs, and he only looked at her ass once, but that was all it took for him to imagine how it would look if she was bent over.

Stop it! You're here to look at gruesome crime scene pictures.

Gruesome crimes, people died, shifter families are mourning a tragic loss, he reminded himself. *You're not here to get laid.*

But he wouldn't turn it down.

She let them both into her apartment and tossed her purse on the sofa in a practiced casual habit, and then led him to a four person dining table in a small eating nook adjacent to the kitchen area. A glance around the tiny sparse apartment alerted him to the fact that either she was a minimalist or reporting didn't pay well, but he brought his eyes back to the table.

"This is everything I have on it," she said as she indicated to the papers. "Want some coffee?"

"Sure," he agreed, already reaching for a photo, intrigued. Used to seeing carcasses from when he hunted as an eagle, the gore didn't bother him as he shuffled through the pictures, looking for connections.

"Are these in chronological order?" he asked out of curiosity.

"Yes, top to bottom on the table."

He grabbed a stack of papers across the table and found an image of the body of a dark haired woman, and searched it over before moving to the next stack and then the next.

She returned to hand him a cup of coffee, but set it on the table since his hands held papers, then waited quietly as he searched.

"I think you're right," he said, reaching for another stack of papers. "Their hands and arms are all scratched up in the pictures and in the descriptions here; scratches, cuts, and small punctures, not bruises. If you were being attacked by a bird you would put your hands up to defend yourself…" He mimed the motion. "But also, none of these show signs of attempting to shift. It must have been done too fast, so the killer was already close to them, eye level maybe, probably waiting for them."

Amy's excitement rose as he spoke. She'd barely heard anything after he'd said, "You're right."

She was right about this! She was going to be the one to blow the lid off this serial killer!

Her! The girl from the trailer park!

She eyed him as he continued looking, sometimes holding two pictures up side by side, other times glancing at articles. The muscles in his forearms rippled even when he reached for paper and occasionally he moved his lips as he was reading. Heat was already pooling in her core, watching this sexy man help her with her case. She wanted to reach out and pull him into a kiss, but she stopped herself.

"It says they were all stabbed multiple times, but no murder weapon has been found, has it?" he asked.

Oh right, we're here to talk about murders. She shook her head. *Am I attracted to him just because he can help me? I don't want to lead him on.*

She did want him to be on her though.

"Maybe it's something he can carry off with him…" he mentioned more to himself than to her.

What if I'm not leading him on? I can date.

Why would someone like him want to date someone like me? She eyed the clothes he was wearing that looked like they cost about a month's worth of her rent, and was reminded of the single mobile home she'd shared with her father after her mother had left them when she was twelve.

Wanbli stepped an inch or two closer to her as he moved around the table, leaning over the pictures now spread out. She could smell his delicious scent mixed with his cologne and her desire rose and flooded her body.

Then a thought occurred to her… *What if he's lying about being a pilot?* He could still be the killer, and now she'd invited him into her apartment and showed him everything she had on the case!

Her hands flew to her temples in frustration at herself.

"What's wrong?" he asked, straightening up from the table.

"I umm, just got a headache," she lied.

His face shifted a little in what she hoped was concern. "It's late anyway and I should go. Thank you for a wonderful date Amy." He was close enough that she could feel his breath on her cheek, close enough for a kiss.

But he turned toward the door.

CHAPTER 7

W anbli gazed out of the wall of windows in his penthouse apartment, windows he'd paid what felt like a fortune to ensure would open so he could take to the sky whenever he wanted. The city lights danced below him, but he wasn't thinking about the view. His mind was on the serial killer, and more frequently than he'd like to admit, on the young woman chasing the shifter killer.

Noticing the pattern of his thoughts, he went to take a shower and ready himself for bed, while he wondered why he was still thinking about her. With his continuous string of dates, many of whom were models and actresses, this was hardly his first round in the ring. In fact, he was so used to dating that by this time of night, he was usually already snoring away, and the date long forgotten for what it truly was – just a night's worth of entertainment.

Yet now, in the shower, as the water warmed his body and his hand climbed down to stroke himself, his thoughts were on the little Asian woman whose apartment he'd just left. He'd never been on a date like that, not one consumed by talk of something other than the general get-to-know-you questions, the subtle interrogations to test the fit or at least determine his worthiness of moment.

Amy was different. What if he'd stayed in that apartment? What if he'd kissed her? She was small enough that he'd be able to pick her up; she'd wrap her legs around him...

He stroked harder and harder as his imagination conjured the image of how she would feel wrapped around him, the taste of her on his tongue, her warmth under him... Would she be hot and wet, eager for him or would she be shy and timid?

Shy didn't seem to fit her, so he went with the image of her guiding him in, ready for him, matching his pace... until he spent himself and almost collapsed, panting into the steam.

Holy shit, I need to get laid.

He could call Tina, she would always be up for it, but the idea was repulsing. Not that there was anything wrong with Tina, but she was just a friend-with-benefits.

What he wanted was an actual relationship. Someone to share a bed with, for more than one night, and someone to greet him when he came home, - but not a 1950s housewife. He wanted someone with passions and interests, someone who could take care of themself, someone who wanted him in their life, but didn't *need* him.

Someone like Amy.

Sure, her apartment was small and sparse, but she was making it on her own, determined to succeed, passionate about something other than marriage and children. And she didn't just want his connection to photographers or agents, she hadn't even mentioned that.

Not that he was opposed to marriage, or adoption in his case, but apparently the women he usually dated only wanted the white picket fence and bald eagle babies.

He picked himself up off the shower floor, rinsed again, then turned the water off and stepped out to towel off. I hate this disease, and I'm just a carrier, he thought as he considered his future. It must be horrible for my dad not to be able to shift.

Able to shift...

Oh my God, that's it!

He had an idea about the case, something that Amy hadn't mentioned so she might not have considered it yet.

And the best part, it was an excuse to see her again.

CHAPTER 8

The next day, Amy took the subway to work as usual, and after the fifteen-minute ride and brief walk, she pushed the doors open to the news building. She was one of the first people into the office, she had timed it that way on purpose because it gave her a chance to walk by some of the reporter's desks and take pictures of whatever they'd left lying out overnight. A useful skill to make sure that she stayed up on what they were working on. She would have felt guilty, but she'd learned the hard way that this was a cut-throat job.

After she made her rounds, and made the coffee, she sat at her own cubicle. If anyone walked in, it would look like she was just reading something on her phone and sipping coffee, not spying on other people's progress. Most of these people were in her position, they were fact checkers, bloggers, and occasionally submitted a piece that actually made the news.

A text came up in an app she'd just recently installed to create a new number, and only one person had that number. She wasn't sure if she should be excited or scared as she clicked on it.

'Hi! I had a great time last night, and I was wondering if

we could meet for lunch. I had a thought about the victims and what might be connecting them.'

A lead!

Her fingers flew across the tiny little keyboard accepting the invitation excitedly. *He can't be the serial killer, if he's offering to help on the case, can he?*

A lot of serial killers get off on the game and the bragging, she answered herself.

It's a public place, you'll be fine.

Yes, but he knows where you live.

As she made a mental note to double check her deadbolt when she got home, a few of her coworkers started coming in, and blessedly one of them was her best friend, Lisa. The petite brunette made a bee-line straight for Amy's cubicle, insisting on the details of the date.

As Amy pressed the button in the elevator to return her to the ground floor at noon, on her way to meet Wanbli for lunch, it occurred to her that she was wearing heels and a pencil skirt, not an outfit she could run away in. She technically didn't need to dress up so much for work, but she was a firm believer in the idea of dressing for the job she wanted, and if the bosses could picture her as an anchor, maybe she could get the position. Retrieving her phone from her purse, she decided it might be safer to keep it in her hand or very nearby in case she had to call 911.

The restaurant she'd chosen was only about half a block from her office and her heels clicked as she strode, but her pace was thrown off for the second or two it took her to compose herself when she saw him. Today he was wearing jeans and a nice t-shirt, but he looked like he'd just stepped off the cover of a magazine, and she almost wanted to cross her legs lest her imagination turn her body's water works on and her panties got wet.

He smiled and waved when he saw her, walking over to greet her with a friendly embrace.

Damn, he smells good.

Prospective serial killer! she reminded herself.

As soon as they were seated and the hostess walked away, he turned to her, his eyes bright. "I thought of something after I got home last night," he started speaking fast and clearly excited. "What if none of the victims 'shifted' to defend themselves because they *couldn't*? What if they all had uniform shifter's disease?"

Her lips parted slightly as she thought this through. It seemed so obvious. "Holy crap, how did I miss that?"

"Well, to be fair, I think I have a different perspective on U.S.D. than most people. Do you think the cops missed it too?"

She nodded, thinking back to her conversation with her contacts and what she had gleaned from spying on other people's work at the office. "I'm pretty sure they did."

He smiled at her with his lips shut, a coy playful smile, and then added, "You have the advantage on them in finding him then."

Part of her wanted to hug him for helping her and believing in her, part of her wanted to run away when he said that, because he sounded like a predator, and she his prey.

Wanbli continued with his theories. "So, if this is the case, all the victims would have had to visit the same place and the killer would have to have access to their information, or maybe he's someone they talked to. I was thinking maybe the hospital, or maybe they all had the same insurance, or…"

"Or the research facility," she finished for him and he nodded.

They were both quiet for a moment, pondering the implications, when her phone's ringtone started blasting out its little bell tune.

"Sorry, I have to take this. I'll be right back, it's a work thing," she said, recognizing the number as her friend on the police force, and she headed for the door to talk outside.

"Amy? Hey it's Mitch," the man started as soon as she answered the phone. "We're on our way to another crime scene, reports of screaming started coming in about ten minutes ago, and a unit got there right away. We were so close to getting the asshole this time! The description sounds like that serial killer has struck again."

"What's the address?" she asked, and smiled as he rattled off an address.

"I'm on my way!"

Amy practically ran back inside the restaurant. There was no way Wanbli could have killed someone ten minutes ago on the other side of the city and made it back here to meet her for lunch.

"What's wrong?" he asked when he saw her running.

"There's been another attack. Can you drive me there?"

CHAPTER 9

"I'll insist on it!" Wanbli answered, standing up and taking Amy by the elbow as he propelled her towards the door.

As if I am going to let her go hunt a serial killer by herself!

He led her to his car as quickly as her stilettos would allow and opened the door for her. As soon as he was inside he punched the address into his phone and took off. "So this just happened?"

"Yup," she replied with a nod. "A cop friend called to let me know. They think it was within the last ten minutes because reports of screaming started coming in around then."

Wanbli's chest tightened at the mention of this cop friend. "That's nice of him to let you know."

"Yeah, I try to stay on good terms with the cops so I can get the jump on things like this."

He wanted to ask more about how she stayed good with the cops but he reminded himself that he didn't have that right yet and it wasn't his business.

"I'm hoping to beat the other reporters there," she added.

"If I'm the first one there, not only can I get more clues, but maybe they'll put me in front of a camera, finally."

Understanding dawned on him and he pressed down on the gas. "You'll be the first one there if I can help it then."

* * *

They pulled up about a block away from the incident, and walked to where the street was taped off by police, and a small crowd of curious onlookers had gathered.

"That's it," Amy said, trying to run but having to shuffle on her toes, in a cute little way that made Wanbli smile.

When they'd made their way to the tape, a frown sank the edges of Amy's lips. The attack must have taken place in the alley around the corner, and the police had cordoned off the area so that no one could see in.

"Dammit," he heard her whisper in frustration. "Okay, let me call my boss and have him send a crew here."

As she pulled out her phone and started talking to someone, Wanbli scanned the tops of the buildings, then the crowd, noting that a news van from another channel was arriving.

"...I'm here and ready if you want me to go on, I just need a camera crew," Amy was saying, but then he heard her voice sink. "Oh, I understand... Yeah, I'll give him what I know.... Alright, see you later." After she'd hung up the call she looked like she was about to cry.

"What's wrong?"

"They're sending Tom to cover this," she answered, and her bottom lip quivered a little as she spoke. "Of course they are. He's a white *man*, because God forbid a little hapa from the trailer park should get on television!"

Wanbli pulled her into an embrace. "I'm sorry," he whispered into her ear. Although he felt for her, he couldn't help but take in how good she smelled, how right she felt in his arms, and how mad he was that someone had upset her. He wished he could punch whoever sent this Tom guy, as he racked his brain for how to help. "Hey, I have an idea. Do you have to wait here for this guy?"

"Fuck him, he's not getting a damn thing from me."

Wanbli smiled. "Good, then come with me."

He led them back to the car and rolled down the back window. "I'm going to shift and take my phone with me on video. I can't promise anything about the video quality, but I can guarantee you're the only reporter with footage of the actual scene."

He was about to get into the back seat of the car to strip his clothes off when he felt her arms circle him, and she pressed her lips onto his.

His momentary surprise quickly gave way to desire, and he returned the embrace, trying to pull her slightly closer still, as his tongue tested its way to her lips, then between them. His eager cock was already awakening when she pulled away looking as though she wanted to say something.

He just smiled hoping that he didn't blow this chance. "I'll shift in the car and be right back."

CHAPTER 10

Amy stood outside the car in slight shock for a few moments. She couldn't believe her luck that he would help, she couldn't believe that of all people, he was helping her. But the biggest shock was that she'd just kissed him, and most importantly, that he'd kissed her back.

She could still feel the sensation of his lips against hers, his skill with his tongue, caressing her, sending shivers down her body, right to her core. She turned to check on him by glancing in the side mirror, just in time to get the image of a well-defined chest, broad shoulders, and chiseled abs. He seemed to be in the process of shimmying out of his underwear and as he sank down to lift his butt then pull them down, when his face came into view of the mirror. Heat flooded her cheeks at having been caught checking him out as he undressed, but he gave her a smile and a wink.

Then before her eyes, his body began to shrink, feathers sprouted from his skin, his muscles displaced themselves and transposed into a bird's body, while a hooked beak, sharp as a knife, replaced his nose and mouth.

She felt her own jaw drop at the sight of the massive

majestic bird in the back seat of his car that gave her yet another wink, and then he snatched his phone that was already recording, into his talons, and hopped up onto the window frame of the car door. With a loud screech, the bird of prey took to the skies.

* * *

Wanbli beat his wings, lifting himself further and further into the sky until the cars fell away and the rooftops looked like mosaic squares. He circled the area several times to ensure that he was alone, and then he aimed for the alleyway where the cops were circled around a body. Catching a breeze and allowing it to carry his gliding decent, he made a slow pass over the entire thing before landing at the far end of the alley.

His presence did not go unnoticed but was met with awe, and he heard the officers commenting about his presence.

"Would you look at that!" said a graying officer.

"Is that an eagle?" asked a younger and shorter man.

"What do you think it's doing here?" asked a female officer as she pulled out her phone to snap a picture.

"Maybe there's a nest around here," the younger man suggested.

"Eagles don't nest in cities, jackass," the older one chided.

"Yeah they do, there was a pair of them in New York City a couple years ago that were all over the news."

"Is this New York?"

Wanbli ignored their continued chatter. He'd really only landed to give the camera on his phone a closer view of the crime scene when he took off, so with that, he launched himself into the air, flying just over the heads of the officers, and clutching his phone still. He made several more passes in the air, and then a thought occurred to him.

If the cops didn't think the killer was a shifter, they

wouldn't consider checking the roofs. In slow circles, he glided back and forth over the surrounding rooftops until, with his keen eyesight, he found what he was looking for.

Amy watched the sky admiring Wanbli, whenever she could see him, until her phone chimed a text message. She pulled it out and clicked on the message which was from Lisa.

"Hey, I checked up on that guy's story. It's legit. The company he works for verified that he really was in Europe from the 1st to the 8th."

Almost as soon as Amy'd read that, Lisa sent another message. "You should totally bang him. Did you know he used to model?"

Amy chuckled and put her phone away. She had known about the modeling from when she'd stalked him, but at the time she'd discovered that she hadn't known him, and figured that he was just a cocky ass, not to mention a murderer.

Now however…

She looked up to see him coming in to land on the empty street beside her, but she checked for traffic just to be certain. He landed with a gentle thud, before turning to face the closed car door. With understanding, she opened it.

Once he was inside she shut the car door again and bent to retrieve his phone for him, noticing that there was a feather beside it. Thinking it was his, she left it there.

When he'd dressed he emerged from the car.

"Did you see this?" he asked, picking up the feather.

"Yes, did you lose it?"

He smiled and shook his head. "It's not mine. I found it on the rooftop of that building." He pointed to a hotel, the tallest building in the area. "It's not dusty, so it was dropped today, and the police didn't think to check rooftops because they're probably still under the impression they're looking for a human."

Her mouth opened with realization of what he was saying. "Do you know what kind it is?"

"It's a hawk."

CHAPTER 11

Wanbli drove away, while in the passenger seat Amy started watching the footage he'd gotten on his phone.

"Where should we head to?" he asked after about two blocks.

"Oh, crap, um…" she answered as she thought. "I need a laptop to get a better view of this, but mine is at the office. If I go back there I'll have to answer too many questions."

"How about my place then?" he asked, hoping he didn't give away his excitement about being alone with her again. "You can use mine."

She smiled at him. "If you don't mind, that would be great."

He didn't mind at all. In fact it was hard to keep his eyes on the road with her beside him in that little black pencil skirt. All he could think about was her climbing onto his lap and pulling that skirt up to her waist!

Focus on the road!

He tried to pull his mind back to the task at hand as he steered them into the heart of downtown where the buildings became taller and taller, many blocking out the sun during this time in the afternoon. Soon he was pulling into the parking garage under his building.

He led her to the elevator as they made idle chit chat, but between the 'Nice place,' and 'You've lived here long?' his mind just kept drifting back to the feel of her skin when they brushed hands reaching for the elevator button, the smell of her, the curve of her hips, that way he wanted to see her naked.

"Oh wow!" she exclaimed as she walked in behind him, taking in the wall of windows and the view they offered.

"Yeah, that was why I chose this place. Eagles like to nest up high." He walked to one of the windows and tugged on a lever that opened the glass outward. "I had this installed so I could shift and take off from here."

"Does it hurt when you shift?" she asked.

He shrugged and closed the window again. "It doesn't hurt per se, but it's a strange sensation that you get used to."

He offered her a drink and they sat down together on stools that ran along the kitchen island's bar.

"So we know it's a hawk, probably one that works in health care," she summed up as he started the video feed, but having seen it in person, he didn't care to watch the video.

He pretended to though.

Instead, he was acutely aware of Amy. He could feel the warmth of her body on his skin as she sat close and he breathed in the smell of her, a combination of perfume, soap, and woman.

"If she fell that way, do you think she was facing south when she was attacked?"

Pulled from his thoughts, he considered the question. "The alley was a dead end, so the only reason she'd be in it was if she was taking out the garbage, and she isn't dressed like the kind of person who would be removing office trash," he replied, referring to the victim's dress and high heels.

"I bet she was walking along this street, and he attacked her when she was in front of the alley so he could pull her in."

"How did no one see that though?"

Wanbli thought for a moment, and then recalled the police pulling out their phones to photograph him. "Maybe he lured her in? People like to take pictures of animals they don't usually see."

She inclined her head. "That would work, and he'd already be in hawk form."

"Maybe we should share that with the police, they could warn the public not to go chasing hawks," he suggested.

She pinched her lips together. "They'd just laugh us out of the building like they did when I told them it was probably a raptor shifter."

He saw her shoulders slump as she said that, and instinctively he put an arm around her. "I'm sorry that happened," he commented, not really sure what else to say, but he was relieved when she leaned into him and hugged him back.

"It's okay, I'm used to it."

He straightened up. "Used to what?"

"Not being taken seriously. People always think I'm a joke, like I don't know what I'm talking about. They treat me like I'm twelve. That's why I have to go through great lengths just to prove myself, like hunting a serial killer."

His heart broke hearing that and he turned to look into her eyes, understanding dawning on him. "Then we'll catch him and you'll cover the story, even if I have to tie up Tom the reporter and hide him in a closet."

She laughed at that, and leaned in to kiss him, pressing her soft lips against his. In case she'd meant for it to be a quick peck on the lips, he pulled her closer, and she slid off the bar stool to stand between his legs. Deepening the kiss, he slightly parted his lips, letting his tongue explore hers while his cock stiffened with anticipation. She tasted like a sweet fruit and smelled like the open skies he wanted to soar through. Her tongue danced over his, inviting him deeper in her mouth and when he accepted, she sucked him in, the sensations immediately sending the idea of what it would be like if she sucked another part of him in.

God, I want her.

On his chest he felt her unbuttoning his shirt, and he followed suit, opening all the buttons of her blouse, and pushing it off her shoulders. Her skin was warm to his touch and he instantly wished all the physical barriers between them to be gone. As he gasped for air from the kiss he felt her pushing his shirt down his arms, and he moved to help, as she let her skirt drop to the floor.

Again she kissed him and sucked his tongue in and he knew he could wait no longer. He reached down and scooped her off her feet carrying her to the bedroom. Their eyes locked as he carried her.

"Tell me if you want me to stop," he whispered.

She shook her head as if to say 'no I don't want you to stop,' and he gently set her down and tried to resume kissing her, but she scooted further on the bed. She reached behind her, unclasping her bra and pulling off her panties, while he dropped his boxer briefs.

Eager, he crawled across the bed, hungry for her, a hunger that deepened at his first glance of her small pert breasts. As soon as he'd caught her, he kissed her with all the need he could feel building in his erection, while one hand explored the feel of her perfectly pebbled nipple.

CHAPTER 12

A my felt her breath speed up as he cupped her and she tried to pull him closer. Above her now, she could feel his hard muscles beneath her hands as she clung to him. His erection was pressing into her leg and she tried to move, encouraging him, but he only continued kissing her.

Not that she was complaining, his kisses were sensual, delicious temptations of the pleasure to come but she was impatient. Part of her worried that if they took too long he'd change his mind, for deep down she could already tell that she'd never been with a man like this before.

As the thought crossed her mind he half lifted her further onto the bed as though she were light as a feather so her head now rested on the pillow, and his mouth sucked in her nipple. She rode the tickling sensation as long as she could and when she was about to protest, she felt his hand gliding over her belly to her pubic area to rest between her legs. With one finger he parted her lips, slipping delicately inside her to tease her until she felt like she would die if he didn't fill her soon. She arched up to him, trying to ask for more, pulling him by the shoulders and he took the hint.

Positioning himself between her legs, his erection at her entrance, he began nuzzling her neck with his lips, his manicured beard titillating her senses and the feel of his tongue on her neck teased her to madness.

Still unsatisfied, she rocked herself into him until she felt the pressure of his first thrust. He seemed to want to give her time to adjust but her craving wasn't yet filled and she rocked herself again until he pushed in again, this time easing back and pushing slightly more. She moaned, or maybe she squeaked, hell, she wasn't sure what her mouth was doing, she just knew she wanted to feel this rock hard man drive into her, so she pulled his hips trying to ask. Her body aching for him.

Finally, he stopped teasing her neck and lifted his head to meet her eyes with a wicked grin that said he knew what she wanted and had been teasing all along. Instead of giving in however, he licked the pad of his thumb and brought it to where their bodies met, finding her sensitive nub and rubbing until, in her frenzy, she thought she may have actually finally begged.

And he delivered.

With one more stroke he seated himself fully and began driving himself and receding, giving her more than she thought was possible and she never wanted it to stop. He pushed faster and faster as the bed creaked beneath them and she felt her body tightening with excitement. His panting in her ear, the heat of his hard body above her, and the rhapsody of their pace continued until finally she felt like a bubble of pressure burst within her just as he gave a guttural cry. Her whole body tightened around him and she grasped him in her euphoria, feeling his final strokes as she rode the wave of her trancelike pleasure.

* * *

Shortly after, Wanbli lay spent beside her. Physically he was in a state of utter relaxation, his limbs felt heavy and his breathing was slow. From the sound of it, she felt the same way he did, nestled in the crook of his arm.

He was happy.

And that made him sad.

He wanted to have this forever, and he knew that a lifetime with him was depriving her of one of the greatest joys in life, and the sooner he ended it, the better it would be for both of them.

She shifted a little, rubbing her cheek against him like a cat and moaned softly. "God, I needed that," she said softly.

He chuckled. "You and me both."

A few more minutes of silence passed until she gave a heavy sigh. "Should we get back to work? That video isn't going to watch itself."

Oh right, the serial killer. I can't break it off with her until that's over. She'll go hunting this on her own and get herself killed.

"How about you start the video, I'll order Chinese?" he asked.

"Is that an Asian joke?"

Crap! I hadn't even thought of that. He pushed himself up onto his elbows to face her. "No, no, I just… there's a place that's close by, I can order any…" He stopped when she broke into peals of laughter.

"I'm kidding! I'm sorry," she said between giggles. "Chinese is fine."

Her laughter was so contagious that he found himself grinning like he hadn't done in ages and he leaned in for another kiss.

I'm in so much trouble.

CHAPTER 13

I t was the strangest and best pseudo date she'd even been on. They sat together eating chow mein and egg rolls, drinking wine, and watching a video that involved a dead body. It wasn't that they weren't compassionate, but as he'd pointed out, their being hungry wouldn't bring the dead woman back. The best thing they could do for her at this point would be to get her justice.

After the first time they watched it, she was disappointed. It did give her enough to write up a piece to send to her boss, but as far as clues went, there wasn't much.

Why weren't there any clues? What could you even be looking for?

She put another bite in her mouth and pondered the scene. If the killer came in as a hawk and gouged the woman's eyes, then shifted and stabbed her, he would be naked when he stabbed her.

"Footprints!" she said aloud. "Let's go through it again, slower and watch for prints from a naked man."

"You're a genius," he said with a smile, already hitting play and adjusting the speed of the video.

The feed crept forward at an achingly slow pace, so slowly

that her mind frequently wandered away in boredom, until Wanbli hit pause.

"There!"

She looked at the screen, trying to see what he was looking at, but he was already clicking around, zooming in on something. Finally, she saw what he was referring to. At first it looked like a smudge in the dusty ground, but there were definitive toe marks, and a heel.

"Can you scroll out a little so we can gauge the size?"

He did as she asked, until they could also see the size of the police boots in the image.

"It's a small foot," he commented. "Either a short man..."

"Or a woman," they said together.

Shortly after, Wanbli sat in his living room, pretending to play on his phone while beside him, Amy typed up a piece to send to her boss. His attention was really on the woman beside him. He found more to appreciate with every moment, from how fast she could type to the way she sat cross-legged on the couch.

"This is going to be amazing," she announced. "What do you think of this picture?"

She showed him a shot that had originated as a freeze-frame on the video he'd taken when he was flying over the buildings. Only the legs of the deceased were visible.

"This way it looks like I could have taken it from the roof."

He nodded in agreement. "Will you get in trouble for this?"

She shrugged in a way that suggested she didn't care. "Not much, and probably not me personally, if anything I might get a bonus." She paused like she was going to return to typing then turned to him. "I promise I'll never sell you out about what you did for me today."

He grinned. "I'm not worried about it. Worst I'd get is a fine, and a scolding."

"OK, well thank you again." She nuzzled herself into his arms, and continued typing on her lap, fitting so perfectly against him. He looked down at her, finding himself content and happy in the moment, and suddenly so sad for when this would inevitably end.

How can I get out of this without being the bad guy?

It would have to be something outside of my control, like work.

Maybe he should ask the company if there were any openings in another city.

CHAPTER 14

Amy walked into the office the next day debating between buying a bagel and wondering at the odds that there would be some in the meeting this morning. She didn't want to spend the money if she didn't have to, but a rumble in her stomach reminded her that she'd run out the door without eating. Because she'd stayed up late with Wanbli and he'd dropped her off at midnight. A smile graced her lips as she recalled the evening. He was definitely the best guy she'd dated yet, and he checked all the right boxes. He had a career, he seemed emotionally mature so far, and it sure helped that he was sexy as sin. She thought about how she felt when she was with him…

Safe, comfortable.

Yes, she could get used to that. She imagined herself sipping coffee at the desk, late on a Saturday morning and while he returned through the window with a fish in his talons, the idea made her laugh to herself.

She usually wasn't one to fantasize or count her chickens before they hatched (maybe eagles would be the better metaphor) but she had something she hadn't felt in a long time.

Hope.

Her stomach protested about its neglect, bringing her out of her head and she decided to go for a bagel. She ducked into the little cafe at the bottom of their office building, and placed her order. As she waited, her boss, Mr. Jameson, walked in.

"Oh hey Amy," he called in his usual boisterous manner.

She put on her best work-smile on and walked over to him.

"That was some damn good work you sent in last night. We're going to lead with that story at eight this morning. Almost makes up for you ducking out on Tom yesterday."

Inwardly she cringed, not at the admonishment but at the audacity for him to bring that up. "Well, if he'd gotten there sooner maybe he could have sent you the pictures, but he didn't."

Mr. Jameson raised an eyebrow at the tone, but looked away to bark his order to the girl behind the counter. "How did you get there so soon anyway?"

"I have connections," she answered with a slight smirk.

"Oh yeah? You think those connections could get you some information on when the city is going to fix all those potholes on the east side?"

She arched her eyebrows in disbelief at the idea. "No, I don't think so, that would be more of a Department of Highways thing."

The tall fat man laughed. "See that's why I like you Amy. You always know where to start looking. I want you to give Tom everything you've got on the killer and start looking into the pothole issue."

"Excuse me!"

He put a hand up as if he were about to calm an anxious puppy. "I'm just looking out for you Amy. I don't want you to get tangled up in this serial killer thing. Women have no place dealing with dead bodies."

Her jaw dropped. "And where exactly do you think our place is?" she asked coldly.

"Don't go getting riled up," he started.

"Where is our place?" she asked again.

"Your place today is at the Department of Highways, and watch your tone with me young lady."

"I think that will have to wait," she replied. "I'll be taking a sick day. I don't feel well, must be menstrual cramps," she added just to see him turn red. Then she turned and stormed out, leaving her bagel behind.

* * *

"Amy? What's wrong?" It sounded like she'd been crying, or maybe she was just really upset, he couldn't tell, but he could hear a busy street in the background.

"They're trying to pull me off the story," she answered, her voice hoarse.

"What? Why?" He was already headed out the door, keys in hand.

"He said something about women shouldn't be near bodies or some shit like that."

Wanbli chuckled at the absurdity. "I'll be sure to let my mom know that next times she's out hunting."

"Right! This is so fucked up."

"Are you at the office, I'm on my way to pick you up."

"Yeah, can you meet me at that place we were supposed to have lunch yesterday?"

"Sure thing." He listened to her recap the whole exchange as he made his way to the car. "It sounds like you have a hell of a case for HR or maybe even a lawsuit if you want."

She sniffled. "Yeah, I don't think it would do any good though. HR won't lift a finger to help someone like me and suing will just ensure that I never work in this industry again."

"I'm sorry," he answered earnestly. "I'm leaving now, I'll see you in about ten minutes."

Anger burned in his chest as he navigated the city streets. He hated this boss-guy even more than he hated Tom, and he racked his brain about what he could do as he drove. Revenge was the first thought, but by the time he pulled up and saw Amy standing by the curb wiping at the corners of her eyes, a new plan had formed.

"So, I have a few ideas," he said as they pulled away.

She pulled a tissue out and blew her nose. "Really? Is one of them killing Mr. Jameson?"

He grinned. "As tempting as that may be, I have plans much bigger than that. What if you go rogue?"

"Rogue?"

"Like indie reporting or something," he answered. "We don't need them to get you in front of a camera. If you just document everything, we can put it out ourselves across all the social media platforms, like a Facebook Live or a series of TikTok videos. All of them." He felt his excitement growing as he spoke. "You'll have full control over what's being said, the editing, all of it!"

She turned to him wide-eyed, mouth agape, but when she didn't respond, he started to doubt the idea. *She hates it, it'll never work.*

"Oh my God, you're a genius!"

The tension in his shoulders dissolved in an instant. It'll work. "I have about fifty thousand followers on Instagram, and I have a friend with massive followings that will probably help us too."

She laughed. "Like fifty thousand isn't a huge following?" she asked incredulously, just as he heard her stomach growl.

"It's big, but not like celebrity big. Want to grab breakfast and form a game-plan?"

"Definitely, but not bagels. That prick may have ruined them for me."

He smiled. "I have something much better in mind."

CHAPTER 15

Wanbli guided the car to a five star restaurant and handed the keys to the valet.

"What's going on?" she inquired.

"They have an exceptional Champagne brunch," he explained, "And what better way of celebrating the first day of your new career?"

"My new career?"

"Independent, investigative reporter!"

The smile that twinkled in her eyes was contagious, and he reached for her hand.

Soon, he was seated at a table waiting for her to return from the buffet, sipping his drink. He'd opted for orange juice since he was driving, but he was glad to see that she hadn't. Not that he wanted her to get drunk; he just didn't want her upset about that dickhead at work all day.

She set down a plate loaded with food. He never would have guessed someone her size could eat so much!

She interrupted his thoughts. "So here's what we know. We know it's a hawk, with small feet. We know the victims are all shifters with U.S.D."

"That's unproven so far," he reminded her. "I could be wrong about that."

She nodded. "True, but let's assume you're right, because we don't have a lot of places to go with this. Would we get anything out of visiting the Hawk Guild?"

He'd just begun chewing a bite of his eggs on toast, and that gave him time to consider the question. "I don't think so. They wouldn't give out information about their members, plus the killer might not be a guild member."

"So that leaves us connecting the victims." She put a bite of steak in her mouth and immediately began cutting another, eating like she was famished.

"They'd either go to the hospital for treatments, or to the research facility," he answered, smiling because he'd been able to relieve her hunger so easily.

She noticed him grinning. "What?"

"I'm just glad you like it," he answered honestly, gesturing toward her plate that was already at least a third empty.

"You were right, it's delicious." She took another bite.

"Good, they serve it every Friday." The thought crossed his mind that he was already planning on bringing her back and mixed emotions ran through him.

Their meal was interrupted by a dark haired toddler, dressed in a cute pink dress, wandering up to Amy. Wanbli hadn't even noticed the child in the dining room until now, but she tugged on Amy's arm, startling her as she was about to take a bite.

"Can you help me find my Mommy?" the girl requested, giving Amy a pleading look like she was on the verge of tears.

Amy smiled warmly at the child and set her fork down. "Of course I can." She stooped down and lifted the girl up onto her hip. "Where is the last place you saw her?"

The girl pointed towards the doorway, and Amy headed in that direction.

"I'll alert the staff," Wanbli offered, rising and flagging down the hostess. Before Amy could make it to the door, a woman rushed into the room, panic written all over her face until she spotted Amy and the child.

"Gabrielle! There you are, I told you not to wander off! I was so worried!" the woman chastised the little girl as Amy handed her over. "I'm *so* sorry about that!"

Amy just shook her head, lips turned up. "No problem, she was just out on a little adventure, weren't you honey?"

The little girl's head bobbed.

"Well, you mind your mommy from now on, OK?"

The girl smiled, displaying her tiny baby teeth. "OK."

"Thank you so much," the frazzled mother repeated.

"My pleasure," Amy responded, before returning to the table where Wanbli and the hostess were watching on.

As Amy returned to the table and the hostess disappeared he saw Amy turn to wave goodbye to the little girl again, and as endearing as it was to watch her act all motherly, it was also heartbreaking. Another reminder of the one thing he couldn't give her.

When she was seated again and they'd talked about how strange that whole incident had been they paused to eat, while he mentally returned to the topic at hand, and pondered as he ate. "U.S.D. usually begins in childhood, so if they went to the hospital for treatments, they would have done so as kids, which would either mean the killer waited at least ten years for this, or…"

"Or it's someone at the research facility," she finished for him.

He nodded. "Yup, but that helps us, because there will be far fewer people there."

"Fewer, but what are we supposed to do? Go around asking everyone if they're a hawk? Would you be able to tell?"

He shook his head. "I can probably tell they're a shifter, but not necessarily what kind."

She pinched her lips in disappointment then took a bite of a hash brown. "Maybe we can break into the office at night and look through their personnel records, if they keep them on site."

"Actually, I have an idea. How do you feel about rats?"

CHAPTER 16

"**B**efore we do anything, let's record a video of you explaining our plan and why we're doing it," Wanbli suggested. They were parked outside a pet store, after calling to confirm that the store had mice. He was hoping for rats, but mice would work too. "We just won't upload it until the killer is behind bars. Let's not notify them that we're on their trail."

She shot him a grin that emphasized her beauty. "A great point."

"Are there any locations around here that would fit?"

She scanned the parking lot. "How about we start recording at the end of this aisle, and keep going as we walk?"

"I'll follow your lead." *I'd follow you to hell and back.*

They got into place and he pressed record, giving her the thumbs up.

"Hi, I'm Amy and I'm an independent, investigative reporter. Behind me you'll see the pet shop, where we're going to get some mice to hopefully lure the hawk into revealing themselves..." She continued to explain their plan, their theory, and evidence thus far as they walked slowly towards the shop.

She's a natural, he noticed as he followed her. *She's going to be huge one day.*

* * *

"You really are a genius, you know that?" Amy said as they waited in the parking lot of the research facility. Most of the staff would be leaving in the next fifteen to thirty minutes, and she just prayed they had enough mice. A glance at the slightly shaking box that contained the squeaking creatures didn't reassure her.

"Nah, I'm just lucky that this case hits close to home for me. Let's get into place."

Amy nodded and got out of the car to give him some privacy as he stripped and shifted, then he flew through the open window again, clutching the phone as he had before. It took only a second for him to reach the rooftop. Moments later he was placing the phone to record the event.

When he nodded at her, she took the box around the corner of the building and soon was accompanied by a majestic bald eagle. Looking at him like this, up close and personal, still amazed her. Logically, she'd always known eagles were large, but now crouching next to one, and seeing that they were the same height, came as a shock. The soft white feathers on his head reflected the sunlight and she could see the intelligence in his eyes. His beak, however, was terrifying, like he was casually brandishing a weapon right in front of her. It was easy to see how he'd be able to rip flesh with it. Countering her impression, he made a soft cooing noise making her smile.

The sound of the front door opening brought her back to the moment. Crap! She flung open the lid to the box and snatched a mouse by the tail, just like the pet shop owner had instructed her to do, and then she gently released the mouse around the corner, reaching straight away for the next one.

Wanbli spread his wings and the mice sprinted into the parking lot, causing two women who were walking to their cars to give little gasps of surprise and sidestep away in their dress shoes.

Hopeful, she shot him a look, but he gave as close to a head shake as she imagined a bird could manage, jerking his head in one direction then the other. The creeks of the door signaled another round and she released two more mice, the result this time was only a disgusted utterance of the short mustached man. They repeated this several more times, and Amy was starting to give up hope as she looked at the three remaining mice, until finally she saw Wanbli's head straighten. Whoever was walking across the parking lot this time gave no indication of surprise, disgusted, fear, or even fondness.

The woman who'd seen the mice was a middle-aged blonde woman who needed her hair re-dyed. She wore jeans, a polo shirt, and sneakers, and rather than the usual reactions, this woman just cocked her head to the side then glanced around her as if checking to see if she were alone. The mouse sprinted for the bushes across the parking lot, still trying to get away from the eagle, the woman didn't hesitate but began chasing it too.

Wanbli stepped out of the bushes and screeched his call, only to have a version of something similar returned, as though a human were mimicking it, then the eagle turned and bobbed its head to her, before spreading its wings and launching into the sky.

He perched himself on a high tree branch about a mile away where he'd be able to watch the car the hawk shifter had gotten into until it turned onto the next street, then he took to the sky again following the black sedan. He tailed the woman to a house in the suburbs, not daring to get too close until she went inside. The house was a quaint single story house that boasted only a dirt patch where the lawn clearly used to be, a light blue coat of paint and faded yellow trim that could use some work, which contrasted sharply with the well maintained picket fences of suburbia in the area. Once the woman was inside, he swooped down to ensure the street name, and then glided to the house across the street where he perched on the roof.

A light turned on and shone through the curtains on one side of the house for a few moments, then darkened again. He waited, watching the two windows that weren't curtained, one a kitchen window and the other appeared to be a living room judging by the furniture. The woman walked back into view, having changed into a sweat suit, he looked on as she poured a bowl of cereal then brought it to the living room to eat in front of the television.

He sat for a few more moments before taking to the air again, circling the property for any hint of clues, and then headed back towards Amy and the research facility.

Inside the car, Amy was wrapping up some editing of their videos on her phone when she was startled by the noise of the eagle landing outside the door, and she exited to open the back passenger door for him. This time she stood blocking the window to give him privacy as he shifted and donned his clothes. She was tempted to peak at that lithe, sexy body, but fought the urge for the sake of professionalism.

Just a glance would be alright wouldn't it?

She turned to the driver's side mirror and caught a glimpse of his tight abs just before he pulled his shirt over his head, and she smiled to herself as she turned away before getting caught peeping.

He opened the door and let himself out.

"OK, I have the address, but she seems to be settled in for the night. I don't think we'll be able to search the place yet."

CHAPTER 17

An hour later, Amy was sitting at Wanbli's laptop again, editing more videos, as he prepared dinner for both of them. It occurred to her then that she felt more comfortable here with him than she'd felt with anyone in a long time. He seemed trustworthy and safe, and she felt herself relax with him.

He'd offered to suvi a steak, and she'd admitted that she had no idea what suvi was, but if it meant that she could watch his sexy butt walk around the kitchen, she was all for it.

"So what do you think of this?" she questioned, turning her phone to face him.

Turning his attention to her, he watched it and squeezed his lips together. "Yeah, I like it, but it's too bad that tree branch is right there," he replied, pointing to the screen.

"Oh, I can take that out." She started switching apps on her phone and made the adjustment as he went back to stirring the side dishes. "How about now?"

He watched it again with a smile this time. "Much better. How did you learn to do all that?"

She shrugged, trying to make light of it. "I had a lot of screen time as a kid I guess."

This time he set the spoon down and walked behind her to wrap her in a hug, as she poked at the phone. "How come?" he asked.

She felt herself sigh with reluctance to think back to those days. She didn't want to talk about it, but then again, he'd been nothing but honest with her, she had to trust someone right?

Time to bite the bullet... "My father was working a lot and my mother walked out on us when I was four."

She felt his expression change, where his cheek touched her own. "Oh, I'm sorry."

Her body tensed as she waited for the next series of questions, that 'why?' and 'where'd she go?' that would each feel like a little stab to heart, the unintended but subtle accusations that she or her father had done something wrong.

"I think the potatoes are almost done," was his actual reply, as he kissed her on the cheek.

She turned to face him, and grabbed his hand before he could release the hug. "Don't you want to know why?"

He tilted his head to the side. "Only if you want to tell me, I don't want to pry. I also don't want you to think I'm uninterested, but you don't owe me or anyone else an explanation."

She felt her jaw fall open in surprise at the candid nature of the response, and then she leaned in to let her body demonstrate her gratitude. Pressing her lips to his, she pulled him around to the front of her as she turned the chair to assist, parting her lips to give him access. She may not be ready to share her whole history of trauma with him yet, but *this* she was more than willing to share.

* * *

Several hours later, after dinner and their carnal activities, Amy lay in bed listening to the easy pace of Wanbli's breathing as he lay beside her. Her bladder and her anxiety about the video editing were both urging her to get out of bed, but she turned her head to watch him for a moment first.

He looked so peaceful and she smiled to herself, feeling as though she finally found someone she could picture herself with, someone who was worth her time.

Not wanting to wake him, she slipped out of bed, tossed his t-shirt on, and tip-toed to the bathroom. Then it was back to work. She snuck out of his room and sat down at his counter, picking up her phone to edit more videos for each social media platform.

Except it wasn't her phone that she'd grabbed, it was his.

And he had the excerpt of a message in the banner that read "Sure, I can move you to Paris or Tokyo, let me know which one you want, they both start in two weeks."

She took a short breath but it felt like the air didn't want to be there and pushed itself out, so she tried again with the same result.

It was happening again, all over again. She'd had an inkling of safety, dared to hope, and now he was leaving. He hadn't even told her about it, he probably wasn't even going to say goodbye, just like her mother. He'd just disappear and there'd be no one to help her if she quit her job... no one to believe in her... no one to love her.

She'd be alone, again.

CHAPTER 18

Wanbli woke alone the next morning. He made his way to the kitchen, expecting to find Amy already up, but she wasn't there, and her purse was gone. He checked his phone to see if she'd sent anything, but all he had was a message from the company about openings in other cities.

He fired off a text to Amy to ask if she was alright, and then put his phone down, not relishing having to make a decision about moving. As he made coffee, he contemplated his options. It seemed it all came down to him having to do one very important thing…

He had to talk to Amy about the future.

Even though they'd only known each other a short time.

The truth was he didn't want to leave her, but then again, he also would be damned if he was the reason she didn't have kids if she wanted them.

His stomach dropped at the idea of having that conversation because it could very well be their last, but now he had a deadline to make his decision.

The urge to punch something almost overwhelmed him. *It's*

not fair! Why does everyone else get to have what they want? When will it ever be my turn? I didn't ask for this! I hate it… I hate it…

I hate being me.

As his thoughts continued on that dark path, he stripped his clothes, opened the window and took off.

* * *

Amy was more determined than ever to blow the lid off this case, especially now that everything seemed to rely on it, and on her, and her alone. If this took off, she could quit her job and go solo. If it didn't, it was back to the grind and the road-to-nowhere. That's why she was pretending to jog around the block of the address that Wanbli had given her.

In reality, she was waiting to see when the woman left, and praying she lived alone.

I wish she'd leave already! Amy wasn't used to running and her legs burned, while her lungs protested. *When did I get so out of shape?* She coughed into her hand and slowed to a walk, deciding that any exercise would probably be inconspicuous.

Ahead of her, she spotted the black sedan backing out of the driveway, and when the car passed her, Amy recognized the woman from yesterday. As soon as the car turned the corner, Amy stopped and pretended to tie her shoe.

She listened to the sounds all around for signs of life in the other houses, but the neighborhood was eerily quiet. She walked up the opposite side of the street again; this time watching for cameras or people looking out their window, then crossed the street again and did the same thing.

Finally, she sat down, still waiting in case the lady forgot anything and had to return, and pulled out her phone. She held it in front of her so she could see herself and hit record.

"I'm sitting in front of the house of the suspect, about to go in and see what I find. This house was found by tailing the car of the woman who reacted to the mice from yesterday. Stay tuned for more!"

With a final glance around, she got up and walked up the front steps to knock on the door. When no answer came, no dog barked, and no camera was detected, she breathed a tense sigh of relief and glanced around her again.

I'm still alone, alright, here comes my first breaking and entering charge.

She walked to the back of the house, already preparing her excuses in case a neighbor questioned her, but she was able to let herself into the yard through a loud squeaky, yet luckily unlocked, gate. The yard appeared as though it had once been well manicured, with a concrete patio providing what may have been a shaded eating nook. With all the cracks in the cement presently, however, it was more grass now than concrete now. Overgrown weeds and untrimmed trees made up the rest of the yard.

Maybe this is for the best, who would expect someone to break into the trashiest looking house on the yard?

Examining her options she saw a window and a sliding glass door, and she cautiously approached the door, still watching for cameras. She tried to door handle, but it was locked, so she moved to the window and pushed upward on the lip of it, it didn't budge.

Crap!

Is this a sign I should give up? Am I really about to give myself a criminal record to chase a lead?

Wanbli would support me, but only until he leaves. He might even bail me out of jail, but after that I'd have to get a menial job in a restaurant or clothing store because no news agency would take me on. That would be the end of my reporting days.

She could walk away from this still, go get dressed up and make it to the office a little late. She thought of the way Tom would sneer at her walking in late, and Mr. Jameson asking about the stupid pothole case.

Fucking potholes! Seriously?

No, I'm doing this.

She walked to the edge of the patio and snatched up a large piece of concrete then returned to the sliding glass door. Holding the heavy piece in one hand she heaved it at the glass as hard as she could, near the handle, and was rewarded when the glass shattered and cement landed on the floor with a loud thud.

She crouched down, holding her breath and listening, but nothing happened. No shouts, no alarm raised, it was all just quiet. Standing up again, she reached through the hole in the glass and unlocked the door.

CHAPTER 19

T he decorating style of the inside of the house matched that of the outside, in that the place was kind of a dump. A thin layer of dust covered the surfaces and the floor. She walked through a dining room that she'd be offended to eat in, and tiptoed to the kitchen that smelled like rotting meat, her heart pounding with the tension. Nothing caught her eye, and eager to leave the smell, she moved to a living room scattered with unwashed dishes, passed a bathroom, and…

There.

A spare bedroom, converted to an office caught her eye, mostly because it seemed to be the only room that had been kept up. There was a desk with cords that looked like a laptop was the only missing piece, a table covered in papers, and a cork board on the wall also lined with newspaper clippings.

Amy approached the papers, reading a few of the headlines of them. 'U.S.D. is God's Punishment,' 'U.S.D. Carriers Shouldn't Breed,' and 'Secretive Forces planting U.S.D.'

She stepped up and skimmed the articles. It was an opinion piece for some news outlet…

Wait, not a news outlet. These were from one of those conspiracy theory sites, all written by the same author, a lady named Holly Cappesian. Returning the first article she'd approached, Amy read on.

Apparently I'm in the right house.

This lady claimed in the article to be some kind of geneticist, but in this opinion piece, she argued that shifters with U.S.D. shouldn't be allowed to breed, and that U.S.D. was a result of years of interbreeding with humans and the only way to address it is to prohibit breeding, a myth that had debunked decades ago.

Amy moved to the next paper, where the lady argued that shifters with U.S.D. should be chemically castrated, then in another paper which Amy skimmed, the author called for the death of U.S.D. carriers to prevent reproduction.

A chill went through her as she read that, and Amy withdrew her phone. Clicking the record button, she hovered over each piece on the wall long enough to capture the gist, when that was finished, she turned slowly, documenting the room. Across the room was another cork board with pinned papers hanging from it, and she approached that one as well. This was a printed list of names with addresses and birth dates. Amy recorded from right to left, until she noticed that in the top corner of the first page, names had been crossed off.

Reading the names on the phone screen, she felt her breath catch. Those were the names of victims, lined out.

And the next name on the list was Adelaar Daniels.

Why does that sound familiar? She wondered where she'd heard that name before for a brief second.

Wanbli's dad!

* * *

Amy ran from the house, no longer caring to be inconspicuous, and tried to dial as she sprinted for her car that was parked around the corner. She listened to the ringing of Wanbli's phone as she breathed heavily with the exertion.

No answer.

She tried again, then again, hoping that repeated attempts would let him know the urgency, but finally she fired off a series of texts.

'I went to the killer's house. It was her for sure. There is a list with names of victims and your dad is next!'

Still no answer.

God, why did I come alone? I should have waited for him. How do I find his dad?

Lisa!

She fired off a text to Lisa saying it was an emergency and she needed the address of an Adelaar Daniels.

"OK, I'm on it," came the reply.

Should I go to Wanbli's house? Or maybe the research facility to make sure that lady doesn't leave work. Fuck! She can fly!

Finally, she dialed 911, and tried desperately to explain to a very confused, rather skeptical, operator everything she knew.

"OK ma'am," the operator summed up. "So you think this Adelaar Daniels is going to be the next victim, but you can't give me his phone number, his address or location, and any information about him."

"Umm, he's an eagle shifter," she added weakly, hitting herself in the head as she recognized the futility of that information.

"I'll pass the information onto the police," the operator answered. "In the meantime, you can go to the police station and file charges."

Amy rolled her eyes and hung up the phone, then started Googling Wanbli's father's name.

* * *

Wanbli returned from his flight and shifted in his living room, snatching the phone off the counter top and inwardly praying Amy had gotten a hold of him. Relief and joy at seeing her name were quickly replaced with terror when he saw her text.

Every instinct in him told him to shift and get to his dad's house, but his human side reminded him that an instant phone call would be faster. He dialed the number and listened to the ring.

No answer.

Try again!

No answer.

He opened the text messages and used the voice to text function to warn his father.

OK, now it's time to panic!

The phone dropped to the floor as he shifted back to eagle form and launched himself through the window. He pumped his wings as hard as they could go as he turned south and soared in the direction of his father's home.

He let out a fierce screech as he flew, out of frustration and with a desperate hope of scaring off any hawks that may be within earshot.

Faster!

He forced his wings to work harder, then he climbed, knowing the fastest way to end this flight when he arrived would be to dive.

What was usually a fifteen-minute flight, he probably accomplished in five, but it felt like a millennia as he flew.

There!

His father was in his backyard, pushing a lawn mower over his grass patch around the pool. The screeching of tires off to his left caught his attention and Wanbli turned to see Amy's little red sedan, taking a corner at a dangerous pace as she sped to his father's house. He looked back to his father, just in time to notice the hawk sitting on the fence. The lawnmower's engine died as his father finished the yard work, and Wanbli folded his wings, and dove.

The hawk spread its wings, talons outstretched toward Adelaar's eyes, and Wanbli screeched a warning again, breaking the hawk's concentration, and causing it to veer off course in its assault.

Just as Wanbli was only several feet away, the hawk flew off in the opposite direction, fleeing the scene, and forcing Wanbli to redirect as well. He had size over this hawk, but it was faster, and the hawk put some distance between them. He pumped his wings harder, trying to close the gap, but the hawk kept climbing; both of them knowing that it could dive faster than an Eagle.

But what would she aim for? She's going to have to hide somewhere?

He continued to chase her through the sky; both of them weaving with the wind currents, and his frustration grew as they climbed.

Finally, he spotted a decent clump of trees in a city park, perfect to hide a hawk.

There! That's what she's going to aim for.

With a last burst of speed, he closed the gap between them a little. He took a chance and dived for the trees, just seconds before the hawk did the same thing.

And two seconds was all he needed.

The hawk tried to pull up in its dive when she realized that she'd basically just dove straight for him, but it was too late. He hit her from the side, his talons piercing her wing. She altered her course again, going back the way they'd come.

But she was injured now, and trying desperately to feign health, but her speed was slower and he was able to catch up to her. He flew above her, matching her pace, then descended until he could grasp a wing in each of his talons. She cried out in pain as he grabbed her and continued to drop them slowly towards the ground, even as she fought to get away.

As they neared the ground, two police cars came tearing down the street toward his father's house, and Wanbli aimed to land in the backyard.

"Here! Here!" he heard, and noticed Amy, standing with his father, a pool net in his hands, and pillowcase in hers.

Slowing their descent, he released the hawk in front of them when they were only feet off the ground, and landed them on the fresh cut grass. His father netted the stunned bird while Amy hooded it with the pillowcase.

"Stand back," Adelaar warned. "She'll shift."

As the words left his mouth, the pillow case and net began to lift, and a naked woman revealed herself from out of the hawk's body. She threw the net off and dashed for the side gate, only to be halted when the police drew their guns on her.

CHAPTER 20

Hours later, Amy was leaving the police station with Wanbli who was exhausted from answering questions. Luckily she'd stashed her phone at Adelaar's house so the police couldn't confiscate it, but she'd promised to deliver it to them tomorrow.

When they stepped onto the sidewalk, Wanbli turned to smile at her. "I'll never be able to thank you enough for what you did."

The corners of her mouth turned up. "I'm just glad I was able to help, and that you got her."

He pulled her into an embrace, but she didn't relax into it like she wanted to. She couldn't. He might not be the safe place to land that she was looking for.

"Want to come back to my place?" he suggested.

She stepped back and opened her mouth to answer, but the agreement stopped in her throat.

Concern grew in his expression. "What's wrong?"

How do I tell him without admitting I read his message? He's going to think I was snooping.

"I… umm…" she started. "Wanbli I need to know where

this relationship is going. I know it's only been about a handful of days, but if you're not looking for a long term thing, I need to know now. I picked up your phone by accident last night, and it said something about a new job." She picked up pace as she spoke, wanting to make sure she got everything out before he responded with an accusation of snooping. "It-was-an-accident-I-swear! I…"

"C'mere," he broke in, gentle guiding her to sit on the curb. When she joined him he blurted out. "I can't have kids, or I shouldn't have them."

Okay, not sure what that has to do with this?

Her face must have given away her sentiments because he pressed on in explaining. "I'm sure you probably want kids, but I'm letting you know right now, that I'm not your guy."

Maybe he's still processing the trauma of what happened earlier.

"I'm not going to subject a child to possibly going through what my dad went through. I've seen too many kids suffer, and I'm not going to put my kid through that, so if you're looking for kids…"

"I don't want kids," she admitted, earning herself a baffled stare.

"Are you sure? Are you really sure, because I saw you with that baby at the restaurant and…"

Irritated at having her decision second guessed, she stood up and put her hands on her hips. "Holy shit, you sound like every male doctor I've ever seen." She rolled her eyes. "Yes I'm sure! I've known this my entire life. I don't want kids. I'm not a 'kids' kind of person. I don't want to take care of anyone else, I like kids, sure, other people's kids anyway, but I have no intention of having any of my own. I want to put myself and my career first, and you can't do that with a baby, or you shouldn't anyway."

He stood slack jawed, never taking his eyes off her. "You're sure?"

"Yes I'm sure, and I'm not going to change my mind."

"Come home with me?" he asked, pulling her into a hug.

Amy was surprised. She was still expecting the fight she got from everyone else – as they insisted she didn't know herself well enough to make that decision, insisting she would change her mind, insisting she was in denial. She froze for a second. "You believe me?" she asked, incredulously.

He chuckled. "Well, you sound pretty certain," he pointed out.

She wrapped her arms around him, returning the embrace, and this time she let herself fall into him, finally finding her safe place to land.

"Are you ready?" Wanbli asked as he prepared to hit record.

She shot him a sexy smile, and he pondered, for the millionth time that night, how lucky he was to have found her. They'd retrieved her phone and were about to shoot the last video. She nodded and he hit record, watching her through the lens of his camera phone, wishing for this to be done so he could throw her on the bed.

She ran through her report on the events of the day, while he recorded it, then together they made a video that included some scenes from his father's security camera.

"Alright, it's the moment of truth," she announced when they had all the videos complied into one folder.

"You're ready for this," he declared, not a doubt in his mind.

She seemed hesitant as she pulled up the first of the social media accounts and prepared to send off the first video. Freezing for a moment, he noticed her pupils dilated with fear. "I'll find it hard to find a job in reporting after this," she whispered.

"What, another job you might hate, where they treat you like dirt?" he reminded her.

Her face shifted to sadness.

"You won't need them. This is going to go viral, you'll be so famous that news stations all around the world will be offering you proper front-line jobs, and if it doesn't take off right away, which it will..." he noted with certainty, "you can just move in with me."

"What?" She sounded shocked.

He gave his best casual shrug trying to downplay the significance of the proposal. "The way I look at it, it's you and me together as a team from now on, and I think we're a damn good team." As he said that, he reached around her to the laptop and hovered his finger over the enter button that would upload the first video. "What do you say?"

"Yes," she answered, moving in to kiss him just as he pressed the button.

The End

* * *

If you enjoyed this book, please leave a review!

ABOUT THE AUTHOR

Joel Crofoot was raised in northern New York state on a large family sheep farm, then left home to join the United States Marine Corps at 18 years-old. After spending four years in Japan as a radio operator, Joel re-enlisted into the bomb squad (explosive ordnance disposal) and was stationed out of California. Two tours to Iraq later, Joel decided to leave the Marine Corps to pursue higher education and graduated with a doctorate in psychology in 2017. After working several years in a community clinic, Joel went into private practice.

In Joel's books you will find elements of both military experience and psychological complexity in the characters. If you like paranormal romance, you will love Joel's books!

Printed in Great Britain
by Amazon

80910324R00051